The Boy with the Helium Head

The Boy with the Helium Head

Phyllis Reynolds Naylor
Illustrated by Kay Chorao

A Young Yearling Book

For Catherine and Mary Archibald
and their parents

Published by
Dell Publishing
a division of
Bantam Doubleday Dell Publishing Group, Inc.
666 Fifth Avenue
New York, New York 10103

ISBN: 0-440-40644-7
Reprinted by arrangement with the author and the artist

Printed in the United States of America
June 1992
10 9 8 7 6 5 4 3 2 1
WES

CONTENTS

Chapter One

A ROTTEN DAY

It was going to be one of those days. Jonathan could feel it as soon as he saw what they were having for breakfast.

"Not Cream of Wheat!" he said.

He could tell by the way Baby Sam

frowned at him from across the table.

"Glumpf da da," said Baby Sam.

He knew it when his mother
said, "This is the day for flu shots,
Jonathan."

And he was sure of it when he
remembered that Duke Duncan was
going to beat the daylights out of him
for sitting on his sandwich.

It was a tuna fish sandwich, Duke
Duncan's favorite kind.

"I didn't mean to sit on it,"
Jonathan had said.

That didn't make any difference.

Duke was eight years old, and big.

Jonathan was only seven, and wore size small in everything except his shoes.

His feet, in fact, were extra large.

"I feel like a chipmunk wearing snowshoes," he said once.

When he put on his cap, which fell down over his eyes, Jonathan decided he had been put together all wrong.

Baby Sam was huge. He was so big that he already wore Jonathan's T-shirts.

He was so fat that he could hardly
squeeze into his high chair.

And he was so loud that whenever
he opened his giant mouth, his
mother came running at once.

Jonathan slowly went upstairs to brush his teeth. Even his toothbrush was extra small. He had to stand on a stepstool to reach the faucet.

"I'll bet Duke Duncan doesn't get flu shots," Jonathan said to himself. "Duke Duncan doesn't even brush his teeth!"

Half the town was sick with flu, but Duke Duncan wouldn't catch it.

Duke Duncan was big and strong and mean and lucky. As soon as he caught Jonathan alone, he was going to beat him up. That's the kind of day it would be.

Chapter Two

THE BAD BABY

There were only two nice things about going to Dr. Mack.

First, Baby Sam had to get a flu shot too.

Second, the doctor had promised a

helium balloon to every boy and girl
who came in.

Jonathan and his mother and Baby
Sam went to the doctor's office.
There was a long line waiting.

Each time a child passed by, Dr.

Mack shot medicine into his arm, helium into a balloon, and sent him happily home.

That was before Baby Sam got in line, however.

Baby Sam did not like to sit in his stroller. He began to bang his fist hard on the wall.

One of the nurses frowned.

Jonathan's mother sang a song to Baby Sam. He only pounded harder.

"Please make him stop," said another nurse. She put her hands over her ears.

Jonathan and his mother tried to play pat-a-cake and peek-a-boo with the huge baby, but Baby Sam stomped his feet.

"Please, *please* make that child be quiet," said all the nurses together.

Finally they rushed the Bogleys to

the head of the line to get them out
of the office.

Baby Sam took one look at Dr.
Mack and howled. He waved his fat
arms and kicked his huge legs.

He knocked over the tray of
needles and sent the doctor's glasses
flying.

Jonathan tried hard not to laugh.
He tried to act as though he had
never seen Baby Sam before in his
life.

"Is this the way your brother is at

home?" one of the nurses asked Jonathan.

"What brother?" said Jonathan.

Old Dr. Mack had to sit on Sammy to give him the shot, and finally handed the baby a red balloon.

But Sammy was not happy with just one balloon. He wanted more. Even when Dr. Mack gave him a yellow one, too, Baby Sam wouldn't shut up.

He yelled so loudly that other children began to cry.

Dr. Mack was in a great hurry to get Jonathan's family out of his office.

When Jonathan stepped up in line, the doctor shot helium into Jonathan's arm by mistake, put medicine in the balloon, and led the Bogleys to the door.

Chapter Three

JONATHAN RISES

Outside, Jonathan noticed that his
balloon was not rising. Sammy's
balloon, however, bobbed high
overhead.

"Just my luck!" Jonathan thought. "What a stinking, rotten day!"

A rotten day, a stupid balloon, a lousy shot, and a screaming baby. That was his life.

At the same time, however, he began to feel very odd indeed.

He followed along behind his mother, but something seemed to be wrong with his feet. They hardly touched the sidewalk at all.

Jonathan stared down at his shoes. He carefully put one foot in front of the other.

Now he was sure of it!

Yes! He was rising!

Suddenly a big hand grabbed hold of Jonathan's arm. A big voice said, "I've been looking for you, Jonathan

Bogley. I'm going to teach you something about sitting on a sandwich.''

There stood Duke Duncan with his two big fists in front of his chest.

At that moment, however, Jonathan rose. Duke's right fist came forward, but Jonathan was not there.

Duke Duncan went spinning around and around.

On Jonathan went until he was even with the telephone wires. Then he stopped and dangled strangely in the air.

Duke Duncan stared up at him, his mouth open.

A crowd gathered below. Jonathan saw his mother turn around. She came rushing back up the sidewalk at full speed. The wheels of Sammy's stroller spun madly.

"Jonathan!" she cried. "Come down at once!"

"I can't!" Jonathan said, more surprised than scared.

No matter how he twisted and turned, he went right on bobbing about in the air.

Duke Duncan stood below, watching.

Chapter Four

SMEDLEY, WHOOPLE, AND FIZZ

The fire department arrived, sirens wailing, followed by the rescue squad and a police helicopter.

The firemen put up a ladder, and Jonathan climbed down. As soon as he got to the bottom and let go, however, he shot right back up.

The police helicopter lowered a rope ladder and pulled Jonathan up. But as soon as it landed and Jonathan got out, back up he went again!

Old Dr. Mack heard all the noise and came out of his office. He was very surprised to see one of the Bogleys floating there above the First National Bank.

"Bring Jonathan down again so that I can take a look at him," he told the rescue squad.

Jonathan came down the ladder once more.

Dr. Mack looked in his ears.

"I don't believe it!" he said.

He called out to the three doctors who worked next door—Drs. Smedley, Whoople, and Fizz.

They shone flashlights up Jonathan's nose. They thumped him on the back and tapped his knees.

Finally they picked him up by the

heels and shook him up and down.

Dr. Mack turned to Jonathan's
mother.

"My dear Mrs. Bogley," he said. "I
am afraid what we have here is a
case of helium in the head."

Drs. Smedley, Whoople, and Fizz
nodded gravely.

"Actually," said Dr. Smedley, "this
has never happened before in all of
medical history."

Jonathan, whom they had let go
of, was floating once more. He
clicked his heels in midair and turned
a cartwheel above the fire station.

"I have heard of water in the ears

and gas in the stomach, but never helium in the head," said Dr. Whoople.

"A very strange case, indeed!" agreed Dr. Fizz. "If it were not for his feet, which *are* rather large, he might go right on rising, and who knows where he might end?"

"Do you mean," asked Mrs. Bogley, beginning to weep, "that my Jonathan is to spend the rest of his life rising and falling like a barometer?"

"Not likely," said Dr. Mack. "The helium is slowly coming out of his ears. By tomorrow evening it should all be gone. But I want him to do as I say."

Dr. Mack wrote something on a pad of paper. He gave it to Jonathan, who had climbed down the telephone pole himself.

Jonathan was careful to stay
around people so that Duke Duncan
could not catch him alone.

The piece of paper said:

No crawling in chimneys.
Obey all traffic signals.
Watch for low ceilings.

"Also, drink plenty of water and
keep your shirt on," said Drs.
Smedley, Whoople, and Fizz.

Chapter Five

THE BOY IN THE AIR

No one knew what to do while Jonathan had helium in his head.

"I do not know what to tell you, Mrs. Bogley," said old Dr. Mack, "but he should be kept as comfortable as possible."

Jonathan said he would like to stay outside.

"I don't want to be tied to my bed to keep me from rising," he told his mother. "But I certainly do not want to spend the time pressed against the ceiling of my room."

The day was warm and the sky was clear, so Mrs. Bogley said that he could stay outdoors.

Jonathan decided to make the most of this strange situation.

He walked along the telephone wires, balancing carefully. When he slipped off, he simply bobbed back on again.

There below him was Duke Duncan, watching.

Next Jonathan skimmed the roofs of all the shops on the block.

He dropped down a kite he had found twisted around a chimney. He threw down a ball that was stuck in a rain gutter.

When he came to the end of the shops on the street, he stepped off and walked through the air to the roofs on the other side.

Duke Duncan tagged along below,
saying nothing.

When he got to the park, Jonathan
air-walked to the trees and bobbed
about in the branches.

He peeped into birds' nests and
startled the squirrels.

But whenever he looked down, there was Duke Duncan.

"How about a game of baseball, Jonathan?" some friends called. "You can play center field."

When a batter hit a ball high in the air, Jonathan caught it. Jonathan's team won.

They played basketball next. When Jonathan had the ball, he simply bobbed over to the basket, and dropped the ball inside.

"This is the life!" he thought. "No Duke Duncan, no Baby Sam."

He began to wish he could go on like this forever.

Chapter Six

A NIGHT IN THE SKY

That evening, Mrs. Bogley said, "Jonathan, play with Sammy, please. I want to make dinner."

Jonathan came into the house. He walked upside down on the ceiling.

Baby Sam laughed and waved his fat arms.

Mrs. Bogley made a chicken pie and a salad. Jonathan ate them outside, sitting high on a church steeple.

He waved to the airplanes that passed. He called hello to the people below.

When he found an olive in his salad, he simply spit it out. There was no one to tell him what to do.

As evening fell, Jonathan bobbed around in the air until dark.

A light came on in Dr. Mack's house as he passed. Dr. Mack, Jonathan discovered, wore a wig.

A light came on in the mayor's house. The mayor, Jonathan saw, had false teeth.

As he bobbed by Duke Duncan's house, Jonathan looked through the window. He saw Duke in his room. Duke had on a pair of boxing gloves. Jonathan swallowed.

When it was time for bed, Jonathan's mother gave him a blanket and pillow. He went to sleep above the clock at city hall.

Jonathan dreamed that Duke Duncan had crawled up the side of the building in the night and was about to slug him.

When he woke the next morning, Jonathan found that he had rolled about quite a bit. He had rolled several blocks, in fact.

His blanket was tangled in the weather vane above the post office. And there below was Duke Duncan, waiting.

Jonathan tried not to think about

what would happen when he came down.

Chapter Seven

HELPING THE MAYOR

The newspaper had Jonathan's picture on the front page. The radio carried his story on the morning news.

The local TV station sent out a crew. They filmed Jonathan eating breakfast on a flagpole.

"Maybe the doctors were wrong," Jonathan said to himself.

Perhaps the helium would stay in his head a long time. Forever, even.

Maybe he would be the first boy to live his life on a flagpole.

If he lived in the air, he could cross streets without looking.

He could watch football games without buying a ticket.

He would have the very best seat to watch fireworks on the Fourth of July.

All he had to do when he wanted to go down was to grab hold of a drainpipe or telephone pole and lower himself to the ground.

The mayor thought of all kinds of things that Jonathan could do for the city.

"Would you change the burned-out bulbs in the streetlights?" he wanted to know.

Jonathan did.

"Would you paint the steeple?" he asked.

"Gladly," said Jonathan.

"String up some lights for us," said someone else.

"Polish a bell."

"Shingle a roof."

"Hook up a clothesline."

"Trim a tree."

There were more and more jobs to do for a boy who could walk on air.

Some space scientists came from Washington. They wanted to see if Jonathan could put on his socks and shoes while bobbing about overhead.

They wanted to know if he could drink a milk shake upside down.

"Chocolate, please," said Jonathan. And he did just fine.

He even saw some robbers, running out of the bank. Because he was high in the air, he saw where they went.

He told the police. The robbers were soon in jail.

"Wonderful job!" said the chief of police. "Wonderful job, indeed!"

If only the fun would last.

Chapter Eight

COMING DOWN

By two that afternoon, however, before he had done half the things he would like, Jonathan began to sink.

By three he was no higher than the fir trees.

By four he was as low as the roof of his house.

By five he had reached the window frames, and by six his feet were touching the ground.

Duke Duncan was there, but so was a brass band. Jonathan was given a ride around town on the fire truck. Baby Sam waved one fat fist at him from his stroller.

For dinner that evening Mrs. Bogley made chocolate soup, mashed potatoes with chocolate gravy, chocolate meatballs, and for dessert,

a big chocolate layer cake topped
with chocolate ice cream and
chocolate fudge sauce.

They listened to the story of the
boy with the helium head on the
evening news. They saw the tape of

the parade, with Jonathan waving at the crowd.

On Monday, however, everyone seemed to have forgotten about Jonathan. The newspapers had been thrown out with the morning trash.

The brass band was playing in another town.

The TV was talking about Texas and taxes. Jonathan Bogley was just another boy with big feet.

But Duke Duncan didn't forget.
When Jonathan got to school, Duke
was waiting.

When Jonathan sat down, Duke
sat down. When Jonathan stood up,
Duke stood up.

Wherever Jonathan went, Duke
followed.

And to everyone they met, Duke
said proudly, "I was the very first
one to see him go up! Honest! And to
think that *he*—Jonathan Bogley—
actually sat on *my* sandwich!"